THE
BEAN
BOY

Ready-to-Read

By Joan Chase Bowden

Pictures by Sal Murdocca

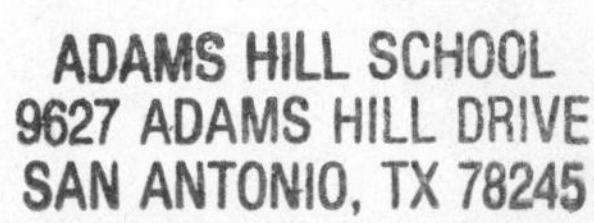

MACMILLAN PUBLISHING CO., INC./NEW YORK
COLLIER MACMILLAN PUBLISHERS/LONDON

Macmillan Publishing Co., Inc.
866 Third Avenue, New York, N.Y. 10022
Collier Macmillan Canada, Ltd.
Printed in the United States of America
10 9 8 7 6 5 4 3 2 1

LIBRARY OF CONGRESS CATALOGING IN PUBLICATION DATA
Bowden, Joan Chase. The bean boy.
(Ready-to-read)
SUMMARY: Calamities befall an old woman who sets out to seek her fortune with a boy carved from a bean.
I. Murdocca, Sal. II. Title.
PZ7.B6718Be [E] 78-12150 ISBN 0-02-711800-2

To Sandy, P.J., Andrew and Dawn
J.C.B.

To Susan, for all her help
S.M.

Once, long ago,
a poor old woman
and her poor old man
were very sad.
They had no children.
All they had was a bean in a bowl.

The old woman thought
the bean was magic.
So early one morning she said,
"Papa dear,
please make our bean
look like a little boy.

"He will be our son.
He will walk and talk.
He will go into the world,
and he will make us rich."

The old man did
as his old woman asked.
He carved a little bean boy,
no bigger than a thimble.

But the bean boy
did not walk or talk.
He just stood in his bowl
and said nothing.

"Then I will have to go with him
into the world,"
the old woman said.
And off she went
along the road.

She walked and walked
for miles and miles
until she met a man
with a rooster.
"Good morning," said the man.
"Where are you going today?"

The old woman answered,
"I am going into the world
to make us rich.
For I have no money.
I have no food.
All I have is my bean boy
in a bowl."

"Then sit here with me.
Have something to eat,"
said the man.
So the old woman sat there
and ate a little salami.

But all at once,
the rooster felt hungry, too.
He looked all around.
He said, "COCK-A-DOODLE-DOO!"
And with that
he ate the bean boy,
bowl and all.

"Oh, oh, what shall I do?"
cried the old woman.
"Please take my rooster instead,"
said the man.

So the old woman
took the rooster.
She walked and walked
for miles and miles
until she met a lady
and her cat.
"Good morning," said the lady.
"Where are you going today?"

The old woman answered,
"I am going into the world
to make us rich.
For I have no money.
I have no food.
All I have is this rooster
who ate my bean boy,
bowl and all."

"Then sit here with me.
Have something to eat,"
said the lady.
So the old woman sat there
and ate a little macaroni.

But all at once,
the cat felt hungry, too.
She looked all around.
She said, "MEOW-MEOW-MEOW!"
Then she jumped on the rooster
and swallowed him whole.

"Oh, oh, what shall I do?"
cried the old woman.
"Please take my cat instead,"
answered the lady.

So the old woman took the cat.
She walked and walked
for miles and miles
until she met a young man
with his dog.
"Good afternoon,"
said the young man.
"Where are you going today?"

The old woman answered,
"I am going into the world
to make us rich.
For I have no money.
I have no food.
All I have is this cat
who ate the rooster
who ate my bean boy,
bowl and all."

"Then sit here with me.
Have something to eat,"
said the young man.
So the old woman sat there
and ate a little cheese.

But all at once,
the dog felt hungry, too.
He looked all around.
He said, "RUFF-RUFF-RUFF!"
Then he swallowed the cat whole.

"Oh, oh, what shall I do?"
cried the old woman.
"Please take my dog instead,"
said the young man.

So the old woman took the dog.
She walked and walked
for miles and miles
until she met a farmer
and his pig.
"Good afternoon,"
said the farmer.
"Where are you going today?"

The old woman answered,
"I am going into the world
to make us rich.
For I have no money.
I have no food.
All I have is this dog
who ate the cat
who ate the rooster
who ate my bean boy,
bowl and all."

"Then sit here with me.
Have something to eat,"
said the farmer.
So the old woman sat there
and ate a little tomato.

But all at once,
the pig felt hungry, too.
She looked all around.
She said, "OINK-OINK-OINK!"
Then she swallowed the dog whole.

"Oh, oh, what shall I do?"
cried the old woman.
"Please take my pig instead,"
said the farmer.

So the old woman took the pig.
She walked and walked
for miles and miles
until she met a gentleman
riding a mule.
"Good afternoon,"
said the gentleman.
"Where are you going today?"

The old woman answered,
"I am going into the world
to make us rich.
For I have no money.
I have no food.
All I have is this pig
who ate the dog
who ate the cat
who ate the rooster
who ate my bean boy,
bowl and all."

"Then sit here with me.
Have something to eat,"
said the gentleman.
So the old woman sat there
and ate a few noodles.

But all at once,
the mule felt hungry, too.
He looked all around.
He said, "HEE-HEE-HAW!"
Then he swallowed the pig whole.

"Oh, oh, what shall I do?"
cried the old woman.
"Please take my mule instead,"
said the gentleman.

So the old woman took the mule.
She rode and rode
for miles and miles
until she met the King
with all his lords and ladies.
"Good evening," said the King.
"Where are you going tonight?"

The old woman answered,
"I am going into the world
to make us rich.
For I have no money.
I have no food.
All I have is this mule
who ate the pig
who ate the dog
who ate the cat
who ate the rooster
who ate my bean boy,
bowl and all."

"That is the silliest story
I ever heard," said the King.
"You must go to jail."

"Oh, oh, what shall I do?"
cried the old woman.
But at that moment,
the little bean boy began
to tickle and tickle
the rooster's inside.

So the rooster tickled the cat.
The cat tickled the dog.
The dog tickled the pig.
The pig tickled the mule.
The mule opened his mouth
and laughed, "HEE-HEE-HAW!"
And out fell all the animals,
one after the other.
They were just as good as new,
even the little bean boy,
bowl and all.

The King and all the lords
and ladies were very surprised.
Then they laughed and laughed
and laughed.

"Sit here with me.
Have something to eat,"
said the King
to the old woman.
"Do tell us that story again."

So the old woman sat there
and ate lots of spaghetti.
Then she told them
the story again.

She told of the mule who said,
"HEE-HEE-HAW!"
who ate the pig who said,
"OINK-OINK-OINK!"
who ate the dog who said,
"RUFF-RUFF-RUFF!"
who ate the cat who said,
"MEOW-MEOW-MEOW!"
who ate the rooster who said,
"COCK-A-DOODLE-DOO!"
who ate the boy made from a bean
who stood in his bowl
and said nothing.

The King loved the story.
He wanted to hear it every day
for the rest of his life.

So the happy old woman
sent for her happy old man.
They took their animals.
They went to live
in the King's palace forever.
They all sat on silk pillows
to the end of their days
and ate only the food
they liked.

The bean boy sat
on a silk pillow, too.
His parents loved him always.
He never walked.
He never talked.
But sometimes they thought
he winked.

Joan Chase Bowden was born in London, England, and came to the United States in 1953. She is the author of twenty books for children. Ms. Bowden and her family live in San Diego, California.

Sal Murdocca has illustrated numerous children's books, including *The Big Cheese* by Eve Bunting and *Striding Slippers* by Mirra Ginsburg. He lives with his family in New City, New York.